Ghosts of Darke County III

Another collection of ghosts stories

Rita Arnold

White Dog Books

Cover design by Ron D'Allessandris

ALSO BY RITA ARNOLD

Dedication

To Mike and my family – Bob, Susie, Ron, Maryann, Joe and Cheryl. Thank you for always being there.

Acknowledgments

I want to thank the good people of Darke County for sharing their fun and interesting stories with me.

To the wonderful employees of the Greenville Public Library a big thanks! All of you have been a great help as I do research on the marvelous county.

Our Little Ghost

Oft in the silence of the night,
When the lonely moon rides high,
When wintry winds are whistling,
And we hear the owl's shrill cry,
In the quiet, dusky chamber,
By the flickering firelight,
Rising up between two sleepers,
Comes a spirit all in white.

- Louis May Alcott

Spirits of the Dead

Be silent in that solitude,
Which is not loneliness-for then
The spirits of the dead, who stood
In life before thee, are again
In death around thee, and their will
Shall overshadow thee, be still.

-Edgar Allan Poe

Introduction

The stories just keeping coming! I am so happy with the way the citizens of Darke County share the tales of the unusual, the scary, the sad, and the enjoyable.

Here are several stories of events that happened in Greenville and near by locations.

In Book IV, I will write about the happenings in other parts of Darke County.

Table of Contents

1. The Motel

Just outside the eastern edge of the Greenville city limits is located some beautifully gently rolling farm land. Here the traveler will find nicely kept farms with livestock and plenty of thickly forested areas providing shelter for wildlife. A nice size tree lined creek gently meanders through this area. Years ago people would fish or swim or even boat in this creek. Unfortunately, the wooded areas have decreased in size over the years as people clear more and more land for building or planting.

In researching the Darke County plat books, a person will find that this section is documented throughout the years as always being a farming area. Then about the early to mid-twentieth century, progress came to town with industry replacing the farms.

The plat maps show that none of the farms were very large in number of acres. Most were eighty to one hundred and fifty acres in size. Just enough land to support a family and maybe have some extra crops or livestock to sell for profit.

The plot of land concerning this story is located just outside the boundaries of the old Greene Ville Fort. Long before the appearance of the white man in this area, the Indians lived and hunted here. Some history books speculate about the possibility that at one time Indians camped in this section of the county while the Greenville Peace Treaty talks were taking place.

Throughout the years it has been noted that farmers turning the soil would find arrowheads and other Indian artifacts. When a foundation was dug for a building, people would find pottery and stones used for grinding grain. This has lead to some people wondering if the Indians lived in this area for an extended period of time. Thoughts of an Indian burial ground being located here have been speculated. Unfortunately, some of these questions concerning the Indians may never be answered.

Ghosts of Darke County III

During the twentieth century the city of Greenville began to grow. Soon new buildings were needed for industry, retail businesses, and private homes.

As farmland was purchased for this expansion, sometimes a property would include a piece of the former Indian Territory. Various history books mentioned that different tribes camped throughout Darke County before the arrival of the white man.

Could the disturbance of a former Indian camp grounds and or burial grounds be the cause of some of the unusual events in this area? Maybe the territory settled by the white man in later years is now unhappy about being disturbed. There are unexplained events happening in this area today that have people thinking that some former residents, be they Indian or white man, do not want to leave or be disturbed.

There is a building (I have been asked not to identify the exact building or location) in this area that is about thirty to forty years old. It is bordered on two sides by other businesses; some of which are open twenty-four hours a day.

3

This means there is activity in this location day and night. Behind the building is a large field that is still being farmed. In front of the building is a busy highway.

There have been many reports of unusual activity in this building by different workers. Sometimes the workers are completing a task by working in pairs when a sighting occurs. Or the workers can be alone and witness a sighting. When a worker will mention to someone what they saw, the other co-workers agree that they have seen the same thing. All the workers agree that previous residents of that particular location do not want to leave.

Day or night, workers will be walking down a hallway when in the distance they see the faint image of two Indians. The features are not very sharp; but they are definitely Indians. They are standing there fully clothed with their arms folded across their chests. The Indians are acting as if they are just watching what is going on in the hallway. They make no threatening movements; nor do they call out to anyone. They do not move, just stand there and quietly watch the employees. Then after a short period of time, the

Ghosts of Darke County III

Indians will simply vanish into thin air; just fade from sight whenever the workers walk towards them. If the workers back up, the images remain stationary in the hallway watching, always watching. If the workers continue on with their tasks and just occasionally glance at the images, the Indians will not leave or even move. They just stand there and watch and watch.

A couple of newly employed people reported seeing the images wearing some type of headdress. But neither worker remained in the hallway long enough to make note of the details. These two co-workers did a quick about face and ran to the office!

Other workers informed these two people that the Indians had been seen several times in the past by employees. No harm has ever been done to anyone. The Indians are just there in the hallway and watch what the employees are doing. In fact some of the employees believe the Indians are there to keep an eye on things.

The Indians are always seen in just one area of the building. In another section are visitors from the 1800's.

In this part of the building, workers have reported the sighting of a lady in a long white dress buttoned up to her neck, with long sleeves and a high starched collar. Her hair is worn up on her head like the hairstyles of years ago. No one has been able to get close to this lady; in fact, no one wants to get close to this lady! The sightings are always from a distance; and the lady is always moving away from the workers.

Some of the employees wonder if the lady in white is the reason for small objects disappearing. There are times when a worker will notice that an object is missing from a room, such as a pamphlet, a ballpoint pen, or a small note pad. After a careful and thorough search, the employee will report the item as missing and order a replacement. Then a couple of days later, the original objects will suddenly reappear! This will happen in an area where not many people have access; and therefore can not play tricks on one another. Now when a worker notices something is missing, they just wait a few days and then finally the item returns. Is this the lady in white playing tricks on the employees?

Who is causing the noise in the rest room? It sounds like a trash can was just over turned; and loud voices are heard. Are people in the rest room having an argument? There is an office in which two or three people work, located near the rest room. People working in the office will investigate these sounds and but find no one in the rest room.

The entire building is a non-smoking facility. Occasionally, when people walk past the rest room, the distinct odor of cigarette smoke is detected. The workers go into the rest room to tell the people that smoking is not allowed in the building; but no one is there!

The building has a large kitchen area which stays busy, even after closing for the day! After the kitchen is closed for the day, workers cleaning in nearby rooms will hear the sound of dishes or pans falling to the floor. The workers will go into the kitchen to check the damage; but there is none. Nothing has been moved!

Other times the employees will smell a peculiar cooking odor coming from the kitchen area. No one has been able to identify this odor. Workers think it is an unusual cooking odor, maybe a recipe not in common use today. The odor has not been noticed in any other part of the building.

A few of the employees have reported feeling a presence watching them at work. When the employees look around the room, a white mist will be seen going past them. This can happen anywhere in the building.

Just like other businesses, there are times when there is some tension among the employees. At these times the ghostly activities become even more frequent and more obvious.

Some of the workers stated that they feel these events are happening because the previous residents do not want to leave. Therefore, the ghosts are keeping a watch over the building. Not only watching but also preventing some changes; maybe this is a way of saying the new item or arrangement of items does not meet with approval. A couple employees mentioned they think the previous inhabitants do not want to leave; that they are happy here and just want to be remembered.

Rita Arnold

2. The Farm House

What is it about older houses that made them ripe for story telling? Are we influenced by the old mystery movies or the novels where the story centers in an old farm house? Whenever I drive by an old brick farm house in the country, I wonder what ghost tales are connected to that house. Are there secrets about that house that only the family knows?

In the northern half of Darke County are many farmsteads that have existed for well over 100 years. On some of these farms, the original house is still lived-in by descendents of the original family; although most houses have been updated, modernized, and have had room additions. In some cases, the house may have had many additions over the years. Still, it is easy to detect that the original house was a basic two story brick building on a stone foundation.

Rita Arnold

The house where this story takes place is a very common type of structure. A short curving dirt lane leads to this house which is surrounded by trees. Behind the house are three old, sad looking barns. One of the barns is leaning to the east and looks like a strong wind would easily blow it down. The other two barns are missing some boards on all four sides; and both show signs that the roof is caving in.

Tall over grown taxus shrubs, lilacs, and rose-of-sharon shrubs hide much of the first floor of the house, even hiding some of the windows.

The trees have not been trimmed for many, many years. A few of the branches are reaching into the downspouts and rubbing on the shingles. On one side of the house, it looks like something has taken root in the gutter; soon a tree will be growing there.

The old house now stands empty. The sad story about the residents is not known by many people today. It is one of those stories that is easy to forget as time goes by.

Ghosts of Darke County III

Until the mid twentieth century, this house stood tall and proud and was always well maintained by the owners. A family with three school age daughters lived on this farm until the beginning of World War II.

The family was very close knit and enjoyed doing the farm chores together. The parents made games out of doing the chores. Every Sunday the family attended the local church with all three daughters participating in the choir and the mother playing the piano.

When war was declared, the husband was drafted into the Army. Since the daughters were teenagers, they were able to help their mother maintain the farm, doing chores, working the fields. The ladies continued to attend church every Sunday and always found comfort singing in the choir. Their love of music helped to ease the loneliness of the much loved father and husband being gone.

Two years after the husband was drafted, the ladies decided to travel to Indiana for a couple of days to visit relatives. Traveling was a rare treat for the family.

Everyone was extremely excited. Tragically on their way home during the early evening hours, they were involved in a traffic accident; and all four were killed. That very same day in the early evening hours, military officials arrived at the farm house with a telegram that the husband was killed in battle.

After many months, the farm was sold at auction to a neighboring farmer. The new owner wanted the acreage to add to his farm. For a couple of years, he used the house as a rental property. After a few years the house sadly just stood empty. The memory of that happy family and their tragic ending was becoming just a part of the local history.

None of the renters would stay in the house for very long. One of the renters reported that he would be sitting in the front room watching television when he would see three young ladies walk past the doorway. They were dressed in the styles from the 1930's and were singing hymns.

During the summer the renter's parents came to visit him for a few days. The three of them were sitting in the front room when a crackling sound was heard. It sounded like a fire in the fireplace; but the fireplace was not in use at that time.

A couple days later the three of them were again sitting in the front room when they heard footsteps walking across the floor above them. Then came the soft gentle sound of a door closing. The renter went upstairs but could not find anyone there; and the doors to every room were all standing open just as he always left them.

The renter decided that he could not stay there any longer. A few weeks later he moved out. No one else ever lived in that house again. After many years the house fell into such disrepair that during a storm the house collapsed. The house is gone and the family is gone. Or are they?

Rita Arnold

3. The Gun

For years and years man has hunted for game, for fun and to use the hides as clothing. At first people hunted with bows and arrows, then with guns. In the early years of the development of this county, people hunted because of necessity, the need to survive.

Years ago people could not go to a local grocery store and purchase meat. Refrigeration was unknown and most people did not have much cash money to spend. A man would hunt for a purpose, for need, and use every part of the animal including the skin. Therefore, hunting to put food on the table was just a part of taking care of your family.

There is a legend concerning the Sturgis family (the name has been changed) who lived in the northwest section of Darke County on the family farm.

Rita Arnold

In the late 1800's, Mr. Sturgis, along with his wife and eight children, lived on a 140 acre farm. At least thirty acres of this farm was thickly wooded and provided an excellent place for hunting. Mr. Sturgis was careful to only hunt when meat was needed by the family; and therefore the woods always provided plenty of wildlife.

The house was a small sturdy two story wood frame building. The floors were a single layer of wood. There was a deep basement with stone walls. The wood floor of the first level provided the ceiling of the basement.

Like many men of his time (and men of today), Mr. Sturgis took great care of his guns. Since guns were so expensive and highly valued, he would spend hours cleaning his gun. Always making sure the gun was stored where his children could not reach it; nor would it be easy for someone to steal it.

Mr. Sturgis had arranged an area of the basement with his work bench where he could clean his gun on rainy or cold winter days. On nice sunny days he would clean the gun out in the safety of the barn away from the house and family.

One wintry day Mr. Sturgis returned from a successful hunting trip. Luck was with him that day because he shot two nice fat rabbits. After skinning the animals, his wife fixed an excellent meal of fried rabbit and all the fixings.

That evening the temperatures started to drop and the wind picked up. So Mr. Sturgis took his gun and a lantern outside and headed down into the basement to clean the weapon. The basement was accessed only by outside stairs. After his wife put the children to bed, she sat in her favorite chair, a wood rocker, located beside the fireplace and started to do some mending.

No one is sure about what exactly happened next. What is known is that Mr. Sturgis was cleaning his gun in the basement when suddenly, BANG, the gun fired a shot! The bullet traveled up through the wood floor into the first floor room.

Mr. Sturgis ran up the stairs, in through the back door and stopped dead in his tracks. There on the floor by the fireplace laid his lovely wife, dead. Her blood was spilling out onto the floor. He ran over to her, got down on his knees and held his wife in his arms, the entire time calling out her name and saying, "Mary - I'm sorry, Mary - I'm sorry."

The children heard the commotion, ran down the stairs screaming as they ran. The oldest child quickly dressed and ran to the nearest farm to summon help.

Because Mr. Sturgis was inconsolable, neighbors and family helped with the funeral preparations. Neighbor ladies prepared the body for burial. Some one arranged the day and time for the ceremony to take place in the family cemetery located on the family farm.

The county sheriff ruled the incident as an accident and no charges were filed against the grieving Mr. Sturgis. As time went on, the accident weighed heavier and heavier on Mr. Sturgis. He found it so difficult to live with the knowledge of what had happened. He just could not live without his Mary.

Three months after the incident, one morning Mr. Sturgis was found dead in his bed. The local doctor ruled that he died of "natural causes." His family and friends believed that he died of a broken heart.

The land is still used as farm land. The woods are still intact and used for hunting and as a habitat for wildlife. Even the house is still standing and providing a good solid home. There have been some additions over the years to the house; but the original portion is still in use. Even the basement still has the stone walls and the wood steps that can only be entered from the out of doors.

There are times during the winter months when at dusk, a man is seen walking outside the house out back to the basement stairs carry a gun and a lantern. By the time he reaches the basement entrance, the figure turns and heads for the barn. The figure then vanishes into thin air before it reaches the barn.

Could it be that Mr. Sturgis is still there, trying to undo the accident, by attempting to clean the gun in the barn and not in the basement?

4. The Presence

Hey, who turned the lights out? What is going on? Who's there? Have you ever been home alone and suddenly the lights went out, or a door slams shut, or maybe a cabinet door will open? If your answer to any of these questions is yes, then you will like this story.

There is a family who lives in a house built in the early 1900's located in the southwestern section of Greenville. This house is located just outside of what used to be the old Green Ville Fort. Near this house is Mud Creek which always has water flowing in it. Also near by are train tracks which are still in daily use after over one hundred years of existence.

Just think of the local history involved with this section of the county. Indians may have camped here, hunted here, fought here, and then soldiers came and fought the Indians. As time passed the soldiers patrolled the area trying to protect the new settlers. Later on a peace treaty was signed between the Indians and the settlers not too far from this spot.

Trains have traveled through here for years and years. First came the wagon trains and then the steam engines both carrying people and cargo to the area.

When the Simmons' family first bought the house in the 1960s, the real estate agent told them that the house was built on an Indian burial ground. The family has never found any arrowheads or other Indian artifacts and therefore just forgot about the Indian story. The father believed that the story was just realtor talk. He did admit that it was an interesting story. He dismissed it as just local legion.

The Simmons (the owners asked that their name be changed) have lived in this house for many years. Their children are grown now and on their own.

That left only the husband, his wife, and the old family dog living in the home.

The Simmons had never remodeled or renovated any part of the house for years. After living there for over twenty years, the Simmons decided to do just a few changes to the kitchen. They put in a new kitchen floor, took out the upper cabinet over the stove and replaced it with a microwave, and finally painted the kitchen walls a nice off-white color. All of these changes were be done by Mr. Simmons who was a very capable handyman. Or did he have some unexpected help?

The first thing Mr. Simmons did was to remove the old wood cabinet that was above the stove. Just as Mr. Simmons was lifting the cabinet from the wall, suddenly the kitchen lights went out. The light switch remained in the 'on' position. Elsewhere in the house the lights remained turned on. There was no electric wiring near where the cabinet hung. Then Mr. Simmons stepped outside and noticed that his neighbors' lights were on. Not sure exactly what was going on, Mr. Simmons walked back into the kitchen as he tried to figure out what was happening. Just as he stepped through the doorway, suddenly the lights came back on! Mr. Simmons just shrugged his shoulders and returned to work.

The next step in the remodeling project was to install a microwave over the stove. While Mr. Simmons and his wife were holding the heavy kitchen appliance in place, one of the kitchen cabinet doors on the other side of the room suddenly flew wide open! No one was near that cabinet.

Then the Simmons looked at each other and stated, "how could that happen?" Their cabinets all had the old fashion snap latches, not the modern day magnetic type commonly used in most kitchens today.

A couple of days later, the Simmons were putting in a new linoleum kitchen floor. About halfway through the job the kitchen lights suddenly went out again. Without even thinking, Mr. Simmons said out loud, "this is our last project, nothing else will be changed." Within seconds the lights came back on!

Ghosts of Darke County III

The Simmons' still live in that old comfortable house. They have not done any more remodeling projects to any part of the house. Nor have they experienced anymore unusual happenings.

But for some reason they believe they are sharing the house with some unknown residents. Both Mr. Simmons and wife stated they enjoy having the company.

Rita Arnold

5. The Mill

While researching the history of Darke County for this book, I found some interesting information about the large number of mills that were located along the streams and creeks in this county during the 1800's.

Some of the Darke County history books I have read report that at one time there were over one hundred mills operating in this county. This includes grist mills, saw mills, sorghum mills(for molasses), carding mills(for preparing wool for weaving), fulling mills(for scouring, cleaning and softening cloth), flax mills(for linseed oil), and oat mills(for oatmeal). There may have been other types of mills; but these are the most common ones I read about in the history books.

The majority of the mills were built along the Greenville Creek and the Mud Creek. But anywhere an adequate amount of flowing water could be found would soon have some type of mill built along the banks.

As you drive northwest on route 571 between Greenville and Union City, there are several areas along the Greenville Creek that look perfect for a mill. Maybe someday someone will come across an old foundation or maybe even part of a building that used to house a mill. Then lovingly rebuild the mill and bring to life more of our county's history.

The subject of this story is a mill that was built in the mid 1800s and located southeast of Greenville.

Many people over the years have related to me the same experiences without any knowledge that someone else had the exact same experience. These are not people who knew each other, nor did they know that other people had experienced the same events. The one thing they all had in common was that each person was relieved to learn they were not alone in what they heard or witnessed.

Ghosts of Darke County III

The subject of this story is an operating mill that includes a gift shop selling locally made craft items and the various grains milled at that location. The mill is set up for the public to take self guided tours and learn just how a mill operates.

I will tell you about Mary's experience at the mill which is representative of all the stories that I have heard. Mary continues to shop at the mill; but she knows she is never alone in the building and will never be harmed.

During the 1980's, Mary decided to visit the mill and look for a special gift for a close friend, something that was made locally and one of a kind. Since she had not been in the mill before, she though it would be a good idea to look around the building and learn how a mill works.

The area had just received three days of occasional rain and even a couple of heavy thunder storms. Even on this day it was still overcast; but at least the rains had stopped. Mary was glad to be out of the house and not dodging the raindrops.

Mary did not see a clerk on the first floor; but the sign did say that visitors were allowed upstairs to view the equipment. The mill was not operating on that particular day. There was very little noise upstairs; and Mary was enjoying having a look around.

While on the third floor, Mary was walking around looking at the old equipment, when she looked towards the far end of the room and saw the back side of someone. It looked like a man. He was bent over working on something, wearing jeans style coveralls, worn old boots, and a red bandanna hanging out of his right rear pocket. Mary walked towards the man to ask a question when suddenly he just vanished!

Needless to say Mary made a fast exit down the stairs to the first floor. There she found the clerk behind a counter and told her about what just happened. The clerk smiled and nodded her head affirmatively and said "oh, yea him again." The clerk then said that she had never seen the gentleman herself; but that other customers had witnessed the exact same sighting in the same location at the same time of day before.

Well, after that, Mary started to relax and even began to joke about what happened. Mary decided she had seen enough of the upstairs and started walking around the gift shop looking at the various items. Mary soon found herself in the back part of the room. It was quiet, no radio or television making noise; and the clerk was at the front counter doing paper work. As she looked at the items for sale she found that perfect gift for her friend.

Before she could get the clerks' attention, Mary heard it. Step – Step – Step. Overhead there were distinct heavy footsteps going across the floor! Then Mary realized that she was standing directly under the area where she saw the "worker" upstairs. Mary said to the clerk, "did you hear that?" The clerk said yes, in fact she had heard the steps before. The clerk went on to say that she wonders if it is a former owner or worker who does not want to leave the mill. The clerk continued that she is never afraid to be there by herself. The steps are always heard on the second or third floor, as if someone is working on the equipment.

Other people have individually related this same story to me over the years. These sightings have occurred again and again; and the "worker's" description and location is always the same.[1]

6. The Cemetery

What interesting places cemeteries can be. You can walk among the tall shade trees, looking at the tombstones and enjoying the peace and quiet. The inscriptions on the markers have changed with the passing of the years; and the stone carvings have given way to fancy designs now edged on the stones. Here we can pay respect to our families' forefathers, our friends, and our county pioneers. Cemeteries are a quiet place for reflection, taking time to remember people and events.

Some people enjoy getting their walking exercise in cemeteries. There is usually little vehicle traffic; and the cars that are there are driving slowly and pausing often. The older cemeteries provide plenty of shade with the old, tall, wide spreading trees and the slightly rolling terrain that makes walking enjoyable.

The cemetery in this story has a large thickly wooded area on the western edge of the property. This provides good wind protection. This old cemetery has been in continuous use since around 1870. The oldest section is located in the middle near the south western edge of the cemetery. The wooded area borders a part of this section. Some of the markers here are leaning; a few have fallen over to the ground, sad evidence of the passing of time. This part of the cemetery is dotted with tall mature trees; and large untrimmed shrubs are found between the markers.

The lane is a narrow paved blacktop roadway, just wide enough for one car and nothing else, really nothing more than a paved pathway. The roadway follows the pattern of the land with plenty of ups and downs just like the old fashion hard ribbon candy. Throughout this section are some large arborvitae shrubs standing tall as if keeping watch over this area, just like soldiers.

The local legend is that if you walk in this cemetery alone at dusk you will have some uninvited company. Be ready for a dog to quietly follow you along the roadway.

Ghosts of Darke County III

In this old section, the paved lane dips down about ten to twelve feet, then raises up and into another section. As a person walks down into the roadway dip and reaches the bottom, they will notice on the south side of the road a tombstone for a young boy.

This young child passed away at age of eight years old, many, many years ago. On the front of the tombstone at the base is carved a figure of a dog lying down with his front paws over his eyes. The carving does not represent any special breed of dog, just your common everyday lovable big mutt! Stop and look closely at the carving. It looks like the dog could be crying for his master, the boy who is never coming back.

As you walk past this tombstone carefully listen to the sounds. Do you hear it? Click. Click. Click. You stop and the sounds stop. Now continue on walking down the roadway and listen. Click. Click. Click. It's the sound of a dog's toenails on the paved roadway. Now slowly turn around. You will see the image of a large mogul dog about ten feet behind you. He does not bark. He does not growl. He will always walk at the same pace as you. There is no need to start running, just keep walking. If you stop, the dog will also stop and then start walking exactly when you start. All you hear is the clicking of his toenails on the pavement. Click. Click. Click.

After a short distance, the dog will vanish. He never follows a person for more then about twenty feet. He is just suddenly there and then suddenly gone. He only follows people when they walk in front of the boy's tombstone.

Is he protecting his master? Or is the dog looking for the young boy, hoping to find his missing companion.

7. The Clock

Many years ago, Mr. Roberts (his family requested that their name not be used) retired after thirty-five years of employment at a large company. On his final day of work, his co-workers gave him a beautiful wall clock.

The clock had a gorgeous mahogany wood case and soft Westminster chimes that rang every quarter hour. The clock face had the old English style numbers, with some fancy scroll work drawn in the corners. The clock only needed winding every seven days and kept exact time. Mr. Roberts loved this clock. He made sure it was wound every week. He and his wife enjoyed hearing the chimes.

A couple of years later, Mr. Roberts passed away very suddenly. When the family returned home from the funeral, his wife noticed that the clock had stopped keeping time. She decided to just leave the clock alone for now, that was the least of her worries at this time.

Rita Arnold

A number of weeks passed when Mrs. Roberts finally decided that she could hear the chimes and the ticking of the clock without tears forming in her eyes. It was time to wind the clock. Very carefully she turned the key, just like her husband had showed her. But nothing happened; she did not hear the clock ticking. And the pendulum would not move. She started the pendulum by hand but after one swing, it stopped! Mrs. Roberts just shrugged her shoulders and decided to have it repaired sometime in the future.

Soon the one year anniversary of Mr. Robert's passing occurred. The family decided to gather at home, for a day of remembering. Also, no one wanted Mrs. Roberts to be alone that day. One of Mrs. Robert's children mentioned that the clock was not running, to which she replied that the clock had not worked for months.

That afternoon while the family was sitting in the living room, suddenly the clock started to chime! The time was 2:00 PM. The exact same time as Mr. Robert's funeral! Everyone became very quiet and just looked at each other. For several seconds the only sounds to be heard were the hesitant breathing of the family and the soft ticking of the clock. Mrs. Roberts looked nervous for a few seconds; and then she sat back in her chair and smiled, saying "your father is here with us today." No one in the room knew what to say. No one acknowledged Mrs. Robert's comment or the ticking of the clock.

As time went on, the chiming of the clock on that special day was never mentioned. The clock only ran for one minute that day and then stopped; therefore it was easy to forget that the wall clock was in the house.

Mrs. Roberts remained living in the home until she passed away years later. She never had the clock repaired. But every year on the anniversary of her husband's passing, the clock would chime at exactly 2:00 PM.

When the children settled the estate, it was unanimous that the oldest son should have the much treasured wall clock. Carefully the clock was packed and transported to its new home. Without thinking about what he was doing, the son wound the clock. He stood there a few seconds enjoying the ticking of the clock and watching the pendulum move back and forth, back and forth.

A few days later he told his sister that the clock was working just fine. She looked at him and said she now understood what was happening with the clock. That was their father's way of telling their mother that he was still with her. Now that they are together again, the clock can now go back to keeping time, and playing the beautiful chimes.

8. The Bible

While Bud was on vacation in 1992, he stopped in Fredrick, Maryland for lunch. Since it was a beautiful fall day and he was in no particular hurry, Bud decided to visit the old historic section of Fredrick. There on one of the narrow, brick paved streets, he found a small store that specialized in old books, newspapers, maps, and just any interesting paper items.

As he was browsing in the back of the store, Bud found a large dusty Bible. Immediately Bud fell in love with the old book and knew he had to have it. The dark leather binding was beautiful, every page in excellent condition, and the pictures throughout the Bible were truly works of art. On the edge of each page was gold edging that had never faded.

In the front of the Bible were four loose pages filled with important Bethel (the name has been changed) family information, the marriages, births, and deaths.

Bud returned home after vacation and placed the Bible on a shelf; and for a time, he forgot he had the book. Months later, a friend was telling Bud about doing some genealogy research on the internet. Bud retrieved the old Bible and the two men started searching for information about the Bethel family.

Having purchasing the Bible in Maryland, Bud never dreamed that there would be a Darke County connection.

After many, many months of research, Bud found that a Miss Lucy Bethel (name has been changed) was residing in a Darke County nursing home. Bud arranged a meeting with Lucy and her niece so he could show them the Bible. Bud was hoping that Miss Lucy might recognize some of the names. He thought it was a long shot but worth the time to try.

Bud found Miss Lucy in her room, sitting quietly in an old upholstered chair, looking very small and frail. An afghan was covering her legs. But when he looked into her eyes, he was amazed at how sharp and focused they were. She held out her hand in a greeting and shook Bud's hand firmly.

He gently placed the book in her lap. As Miss Lucy opened the Bible, her hands began to tremble and she could not speak. When she saw the pages with the old family names, tears quietly ran down her cheeks. She could not see for a few minutes as her eyes were swimming in moisture.

The room was quiet, very quiet. No one said a word. Then Lucy's niece softly explained to Bud the history of the old Bible.

Miss Lucy had always lived in Darke County. She grew up on a farm. After her parents passed away, Miss Lucy inherited the farm. She continued to live there many years managing the farm. Then the time came when she could no longer live alone; and she decided to move into a nursing home.

Miss Lucy was always very close to her family. Many years ago when Lucy had to sell the farm house and most of the contents, the Bible was accidentally placed in the auction. It broke Miss Lucy's heart to think that the Bible would no longer be with her or in the family.

The entire time that Miss Lucy's niece was talking, Bud noticed that Miss Lucy never took her eyes off the Bible. Her hands continued to softly caress the Bible. At one point she raised her eyes to look out her window. Her face had a certain glow to it; a small smile was on her mouth, and a sparkle in her eyes. Bud knew immediately what he wanted to do, what he had to do.

That night as Miss Lucy fell asleep in her room, the Bible was on the nightstand next to her bed and a smile on her face.

9. The Travelers

The year is 1931 and Liberty Township is a rural developing area of farms and the occasional small cluster of stores and houses at a crossroads.

One spring evening at around dusk two young boys were walking home along a dusty, lonely road after moving the cows to a new pasture. Being typical boys they just meandered along the road, walking and talking, kicking at stones, and throwing the occasional stick.

Suddenly, Billy grabbed his big brother Tommy's (the names and location have been changed) arm and they both stopped walking and just stared. Billy pointed straight ahead of them at the strangest sight the boys have ever seen.

At that particular moment the boys saw a brightly painted wooden, square-topped, enclosed wagon with a stove pipe coming out of the top. With each step of the horse, the boys only became more rooted to the road. Pulling the wagon was a worn out old horse just slowly plodding along kicking up the dust from the road. Sitting up on the wagon seat was a man holding the reins who motioned for the boys to come over to the wagon.

The boys slowly and carefully walked towards the wagon as if hypnotized or in a trance. As they got closer, the boys noticed that the wagon driver wore a brightly colored shirt with baggy sleeves, a bandana around his head, and bright shinny rings on his fingers. The woman sitting beside him wore a bold, bright colored dress and lots of jewelry.

About twenty feet from the wagon, Tommy grabbed Billy's right hand and started pulling him backwards. After stumbling backward just a few feet, the boys quickly turned and took off at a dead run, moving just as fast as their short legs could carry them. The boys headed in the opposite direction from the wagon and went to the closest neighbors' house.

Ghosts of Darke County III

By the time boys reached the neighbors' house, they were gasping for air and white as a sheet. The neighbor gently calmed the boys down and talked with them about what they just witnessed. Smiling, he thought the boys just had a wild imagination but decided it best to walk the boys home.

The neighbor talked with the boys' parents about what happened and explained why he walked them home. The adults just chuckled about the entire episode and soon sent the boys to bed.

The next day the boys talked privately about what happened the night before. That is when they realized that the wagon never made a sound even though the wagon was slowly moving towards them. They never heard the sound of the wagon wheels or the horse's harness. Billy said that they saw the ghost wagon.

At that time there was a legend in that area that every spring a ghost wagon would appear traveling slowly down that same road, in the same direction, at the same time of day.

The description of the wagon and the people would always be the same. People of all ages would report seeing the ghost wagon and horse but none of them ever heard a sound! Not one single sound!

Years ago small bands of people would travel through this area every spring. They would camp somewhere in an isolated location in the township. Usually they would find a wooded area near some flowing water, and as far away from established settlers as possible. The travelers claimed they were looking for work. But none of the local farmers or shopkeepers could recall being asked by the travelers about any type of employment.

After about a week the travelers would move on. No one ever saw them leave. They would be there one day and suddenly gone the next. Some of the farmers would begin to notice that small hand tools were missing from their barns. The ladies would find that clothing items had been taken from their wash line; and the shopkeepers found that various items were missing from their stores.

Finally one year the citizens banded together and watched for the travelers. Just like clock work, one bright spring day the wagons came rolling down the road into the township. Only this time the citizens made sure that the travelers moved on into Indiana without stopping in their township.

The head of the traveling band yelled at the citizens that they would come back every spring; and no one could stop them. Maybe the ghost wagon is their way of keeping that promise.

Rita Arnold

10. The Wreck

In November, 1917, at about dusk there was an automobile wreck on the West Milton Pike (today known as State Route 571) at a sharp curve a couple of miles or so east of Greenville. This was a time period when the automobiles were gaining in popularity but not very common, especially in rural areas. The cars had to share the roadways with horse and buggies. It was common for cars and buggies to move to the side of the road and make way for each other.

The Arnett family was returning from a trip to Dayton where they had been visiting with family. In the car were Mr. and Mrs. Arnett, a teenage son, and their infant grandchild. The newspaper account stated that Mr. Arnett pulled over to the side of the road to allow a horse and buggy plenty room to pass as they traveled in the opposite direction.

Darkness was setting in; and in those days the vehicles did not have very strong headlights. Mr. Arnett probably could not see very far ahead of the car or much to the side of the road.

As the car approached a sharp curve, Mr. Arnett slowed down; and then noticed a buggy coming in the opposite direction at a slow speed. He carefully pulled the car over to the side of the roadway and stopped; therefore, allowing the buggy plenty of room to pass and, also, so the car would not spook the horse.

Maybe because the daylight was fading, or maybe because Mr. Arnett could not see the side of the road clearly, or perhaps he was just plain tired from the long day of traveling. No one is sure just why or exactly how the accident happened.

As Mr. Arnett pulled slowly over, the right front tire started going down the steep embankment pulling the rest of the car into the ditch. The vehicle rolled over and landed on its top tossing the occupants around inside the car.

Ghosts of Darke County III

The children and Mrs. Arnett escaped with only bruises and some minor cuts. Unfortunately Mr. Arnett was not so lucky. He was pinned underneath the car, his skull crushed, dying instantly.

A few days later when Mrs. Arnett was able to talk about the wreck, she stated that her husband was blinded by the glare of headlights from an on coming car. She maintained that a large automobile was moving at a high rate of speed, hit their car and continued on without stopping. She did not remember seeing a buggy on the road. Regardless of the exact cause of the accident, the result was a tragic lost of life.

Could this accident be the reason for some unusual ghostly happenings at this location?

Some of the residents who live along this stretch of the highway have reported hearing faint screams and moaning, as if someone was hurt and needed help. These sounds only occur at night in the month of November.

Other people have stated that at dusk they see the faint, misty-like figures of people moving about beside the road. The people are dressed in the clothing styles of the early 1900's but their feet make no sound on the ground. It is as if the figures are slowly floating. If you get too close to the people, they will simply vanish right before your eyes.

Are these the accident victims looking for help? Or are they just trying to understand what has suddenly happened to them to change their lives forever?[1]

11. The Waiting

On a peaceful summer evening a few years ago, while walking along north on Columbia Street in Union City, Sara (name has been changed) noticed a dim light in the third floor window of an old abandoned house. At the same moment she noticed movement in that window, the shadow of a person pacing.

Feeling uneasy about the situation, Sara began walking as fast as her legs could carry her away from the house. She took the shortest way home, cutting through a neighbor's yard. Thankfully she only had four blocks to go. But those four blocks soon felt like four miles to Sara.

At home Sara's husband was watching television in the family room. Sara ran through the house to find him and was gasping for air when she finally reached that room.

Her husband soon got her to calm down enough to tell him exactly what had happened. After telling him the entire story, her husband decided to notify the local police about what had happened. Both Sara and her husband thought that probably someone had broken into the house with the intent of trying to scare people.

A couple days later while in town shopping, Sara stopped at the police station and asked what they had found at the house. The officer stated that every door was locked and there was no evidence of a break-in.

Sara knew that her imagination was not overly active, nor was she crazy, and that she really did see something in that window. She just was not sure who to talk to about this event. Finally she decided to just forget the whole episode.

A few weeks later Sara was having lunch with a friend at a local restaurant. Her friend lowered her voice and in a hushed tone started telling Sara what she saw while walking the night before.

Ghosts of Darke County III

Her friend saw a soft light in the third floor window of a house on Columbia Street. While looking at the lighted window, she saw what looked like someone walking slowly past the window. This turned out to be the same house and the same time of day as Sara's incident. Soon Sara and her friend decided that they just had to learn the history of that house.

For years and years Union City was a town accustomed to train traffic. Freight trains and passenger trains were very common running through this town. Many of the towns' residents made their living working for the railroad companies.

In this particular house lived a brakeman named Charles, for the D. G. & U. line. Charles and his wife had been very happily married for many years. After all those years she was always eager for Charles to return home from work. Whenever Charles left for work on the train, he never failed to tell his wife to leave a light on in the upstairs window. This was because he could see the light all the way from the train tracks. And the light made him happy that his lovely wife was waiting for him.

This was a time period when most people still used oil lamps to light their houses. These would give off a soft, faint light.

One evening she was standing by the upstairs windows with the oil lamp lighting the room. Hearing a knock on the front door, she hurried downstairs to see who it could be. It was a solemn looking gentleman from the train company informing her that there had been a train wreck and her husband was killed instantly.

She let out a scream and yelled "no, that's not possible; he said that he would be back." She ran back upstairs to wait for her husband, but Charles did not return from work. His wife became inconsolable. She soon became despondent and died. The doctor who examined the body ruled that she died of natural causes. Her friends and family disagreed with him and said that she died of a broken heart.

Ghosts of Darke County III

Could it be that she is still putting a light in the upstairs window waiting for Charles to come home?

Rita Arnold

12. The Lonely

This is a story that has its beginning back in the mid 1800s. The year is 1865. A Mr. Frank McWhinney moved from Preble County to the New Madison area; and soon after that he moved on north to Greenville. For thirty-five years he worked as the agent for the Pan Handle Railroad Company. Many newspaper articles have reported that during his life time he was involved in the construction of many of Greenville's commercial buildings and even some of the grand residences.

During the late 1800's he became involved in banking and soon owned one of the largest and most prominent Greenville banks. It was during this time period that he moved his family into a large residence at Fifth and Broadway for which he paid the enormous sum of twenty thousand dollars.

When looking at the pictures of this house you can just imagine the stylish interior with the high ceilings, the wood trim around the doorways and windows, the fancy crown molding, the wood floors in each room, and of course, a wood stairway with a decorative hand railing. Maybe the house had its own character, some uneven floors, doors that would occasionally stick due to weather changes, or possibly a creaky step in the stairway that signals to the occupants when someone was on the stairs and on which step.

It is documented that the house had a large tank in the attic which collected rain water from the roof. This water then traveled through pipes to bathtubs located on the upper floor. This was very advanced plumbing for its time. Most people were still carrying water from an outside pump, heating it on a stove, and then filling their bathtubs bucket by bucket.

The McWhinney's had two daughters, one who grew to womanhood and married a Greenville attorney. The other daughter led a much sadder life.

Ghosts of Darke County III

Laura, at age 15, suffered from typhoid fever which left her partially paralyzed for the rest of her life. She lived the next thirty-two years with her parents and her disability in that large house.

No where could I find it documented that she joined any of the social clubs nor was there any mention of her having participated in her church activities. Did she dream of male companionship like her sister had found? Did she have someone special that filled her everyday thoughts? Was she a sad, lonely lady?

In 1898, at age forty-seven, Laura decided that she could not continue living. On a Thursday afternoon, after the dinner hour, she went up the stairs to her room while her mother remained downstairs. Laura proceeded to remove her clothes, putting on a long white night gown; she went up to the attic. There she climbed the step ladder beside the water tank, carefully removed the lid and jumped in, thus ending her life in six feet of cold water. A sad, sad, end to a sad life.

By 1918 both Mr. and Mrs. McWhinney had passed away. The house was sold to settle the estate and shortly thereafter was torn down.

Soon a movie theatre was built on that lot. In 1919, Tony and Sante Macci opened the Wayne Theatre.

Could the tragic ending to Laura McWhinney's life explain the unusual events that are reported to happen in the theatre?

Some of the former theatre employees have told me of interesting and unexplainable happenings. No one has ever been harmed; but some people have been made very uneasy and will not walk into certain areas alone.

One employee was in the lunch room by herself, eating when suddenly she heard some distant, soft whistling. She looked out the doorway and found no one there. While she finished eating, she thought what a strange tune, definitely not a current, popular tune. She needed to return to work and put the whole episode out of her mind. A few weeks later the whistling returned with the same tune in the same area at the same time of day.

Not wanting to sound crazy, the employee decided not to tell anyone. Then one day, another employee asked her if she heard the whistling in that area of the building. After a short discussion they learned that they had heard the same tune on different days and always when they were alone. Neither employee recognized the tune. As time went on more and more of the employees admitted to hearing the soft whistling. Then one day an employee recognized the tune. It was a favorite song of his great grandmother when she was a young girl – in the late 1800's!

Who is the lady in the light pink dress? Only young children have reported seeing a lady standing in a doorway watching. They all give the same description that she just stands there, watching, in a floor length light pink dress with long sleeves and a smile on her face. Is this Laura McWhinney dreaming of the children she never had? Does she want to be around people?

Rita Arnold

No one has figured out the reason that the projector, which is in excellent condition, breaks down so frequently. New film in perfect condition will break. And then there are the times when parts will fall off the projector when no one is near the machine.

The McWhinney house may be gone, but are the people still there?[2]

13. The Jail

In Greenville, there is an alley connecting 4th. and 5th. Streets, paralleling Broadway and located between Broadway and Sycamore. Business trucks use this alley for making deliveries to the retail stores. Sometimes you will find county and city vehicles parked along the alley as employees go about their business. But there are those few times, usually in the evening, when there is no auto traffic using the alley and very few people around, when unusual noises and sights will happen.

After the Civil War ended, Greenville began to grow and the need for a jail became apparent. In 1869 to 1870 the county jail was built with a sheriff's residence attached. The cost to the county was a grand total of $39,750 dollars – for the residence and jail.

Rita Arnold

This complex was located next to the courthouse on the south side facing Broadway. The residence was nearest the street with a small grassy area between the building and the sidewalk. The jail portion was located behind the residence with an outside entrance facing the alley and a connecting doorway between the buildings.

The years passed with many people requiring the use of the jail. The building was only about ten years old when one of the then most famous local citizens occupied a jail cell that was Monroe Robinson, in 1879.

Robinson was arrested and later found guilty of murdering his brother-in-law, Wiley Coulter on October 23, 1879 in Riptown (now known as Painter's Creek) and sentenced to death by hanging. C. M. Anderson, attorney for Robinson, did everything he could to prevent the hanging. He even submitted an application to the Governor of Ohio to have the sentence commuted to imprisonment for life. All Mr. Anderson was able to do was procure for Robinson an 86 day respite.

Ghosts of Darke County III

During July, 1880, Monroe Robinson wrote a series of letters to the editor of *The Greenville Journal.*

Robinson thanked his attorney for being a caring man and asked that he see to Robinson's burial. The rest of the letters talked about Monroe's life as he was growing up working various jobs and never making much money. The last couple of letters discussed his wife and children. He complained that they did not understand him or love him. Monroe blamed them and others for all his problems. He never apologized for beating his wife or for letting his children go hungry while he went out drinking.

Until the time of his hanging, he never accepted responsibility for his actions. The day of the hanging, his oldest son came to see him in jail. Robinson was mad because his wife and children had testified against him. Monroe spent the entire visit ranting and raving at the boy, blaming him for Monroe's problems. Quietly the boy left the jail crying.

Rita Arnold

Then a minister came to spend time with Monroe and to pray with him. Finally, the only person left was Monroe's attorney who promised to make the burial arrangements.

Sheriff Runkle then came into the cell and read aloud the death warrant during which time Monroe cursed and yelled about the devil possessing his family.

Monroe Robinson began his last walk as he was lead from the cell into the jail yard. Slowly, with his hands tied behind his back, he carefully climbed the steps of the wooden scaffold, one at a time. Step. Step. Step. The higher he went the more quiet the crowd became, who gathered to watch the event. The noose was carefully placed around his neck. Then at twelve noon Monroe Robinson was hanged. The crowd gasped! No one spoke.

Robinson was dead. The crowd started to leave the area. Some went to visit with friends, some went to church to pray for his soul, and others just went home. But no one forgot what they had witnessed on that day in Greenville.

Ghosts of Darke County III

But did everyone leave the area? Many people have told about walking through the alley, passing the area where the old jail was located, and hearing some unusual sounds.

Some people have reported hearing what sounds like a large crowd that has gathered the faint sound of muffled voices and the shuffling of feet. But no one is there. Other people have heard what sounds like a man talking non-stop, almost like he is mad about something. But no one is there. Still other people have talked of walking along the alley and suddenly they walk through a cold spot. Even on a hot summer day, the cold spot can cause a person to stop and shiver.

Then there are the people who are walking alone through the alley and hear footsteps. Not the type of steps you hear on cement, but the sound of someone walking up wooden steps! People look around and realize – there are no wooden steps in the area!!

Is Monroe Robinson still in the jail yard? Is he still blaming others for his arrest?

Rita Arnold

References

Chapter 5 The Mill
1. "The Boockeye State," *The Dayton Daily News,* (October 10, 2003).

Chapter 10 The Wreck
1. "The Greenville Democrat," (November 7, 1917).

Chapter 12 The Lonely
1. "The Greenville Journal," June 23, 1910).

Rita Arnold

Our Little Ghost

A winsome little ghost it is,
Rosy-checked and bright of eye;
With yellow curls all breaking loose
From the small cap pushed awry.
Up it climbs among the pillows,
For the "big dark" brings no dread,
And a baby's boundless fancy
Makes a kingdom of a bed.

-Louis May Alcott

_____

Ghosts of Darke County III

Rita Arnold